Caroline Wells Healey Dall

Barbara Fritchie

Caroline Wells Healey Dall

Barbara Fritchie

ISBN/EAN: 9783337038977

Printed in Europe, USA, Canada, Australia, Japan

Cover: Foto ©Andreas Hilbeck / pixelio.de

More available books at **www.hansebooks.com**

BARBARA FRITCHIE.

FROM A PHOTOGRAPH BY BYERLY.

BARBARA FRITCHIE

A Study

BY

CAROLINE H. DALL

AUTHOR OF

"THE COLLEGE, MARKET, AND COURT," "WHAT WE REALLY KNOW
ABOUT SHAKESPEARE," "THE LIFE OF ANANDABAI JOSHEE"
"LETTERS HOME FROM COLORADO, UTAH, AND
CALIFORNIA," ETC., ETC.

Honor to her, and let a tear
Fall for her sake on Stonewall's bier
J. G. WHITTIER

BOSTON
ROBERTS BROTHERS
1892

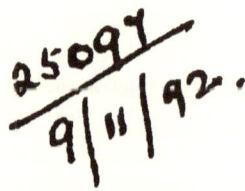

PREFACE.

(History of the Poem, and the reason why these pages
have been written.)

IN December, 1862, a great-nephew
of John Caspar Fritchie, returning
to Washington after an extended bridal
tour, went to Frederick to visit his relatives, and arrived just in time to attend
Barbara Fritchie's funeral.

The account of the funeral, published
in the local Union paper, naturally stimulated the memories of the German residents, and Barbara's various exploits
were related.

The story of September 6th interested
her nephew, and on returning to his
Georgetown home he repeated it to a
brother.

This brother, a well-known real-estate agent in Washington, was on intimate terms with Mrs. Southworth the novelist.

Mrs. Southworth was just recovering from a severe illness, and her friend told her the story as he heard it. The statement was informal. Nothing was known or said about Jackson's ordering his troops to fire. The troops fired; Barbara waved the flag which the firing threw down, reproaching the men for their disloyalty, and the stern voice of the general cried, "March on!"

The vivid imagination of Mrs. Southworth saw the possibilities of this touching story, and she wrote her letter to Whittier. Whittier was fired by its noble suggestions; and ignorant of Frederick, of its local possibilities, of the constant irregular firing upon the flag which went on in its streets and neighborhood, gave his imagination full play. It was natural that he should think

that the general who gave the order to
" March on ! " was at his post when the
disturbance began. Hardly had the ballad been printed before the truth of the
story began to be questioned in Maryland and Virginia ; and as the rumors
of denial grew louder and louder, Miss
Dix, from her post in the hospitals, wrote
to the poet, reaffirming the facts.

The two parties misunderstood each
other. What irritated the Southerners
was the assertion that their favorite
general ordered his men to fire on an
aged woman. The Northerner, proud of
the courageous Barbara, and indifferent
to Jackson, supposed it was the woman's
heroism that offended, and so nothing
was established ; and quite lately Whittier told a friend residing in Baltimore
that he very much regretted the ballad,
as he now doubted the story, and that it
was the only thing he had ever written

for the truth of which he could not vouch.

Here the fishermen of Marblehead step up to remind him of Ffloyd Ireson!

But Whittier has no occasion to regret his ballad. Noble-hearted Stonewall Jackson neither loses nor gains by the story, and would willingly spare a laurel-leaf in the brave old German's honor.

In 1876, fourteen years after the events related, I went to Frederick, and satisfied myself that the story was true as regarded Barbara. I interviewed Valerius Ebert, in whose possession I found her flag, the photographer Byerly, Mrs. Handshew, and other connections of Caspar Fritchie; but I relied chiefly upon Dr. Lewis H. Steiner, late librarian of the Enoch Pratt Library, for the details which filled out the story.

In March, 1878, I published the story, as I understood it, in a magazine printed

at Springfield, Massachusetts, and called
" Sunday Afternoon."

Owing to the facts that feelings were
still exasperated, and Dr. Steiner's home
still in Frederick, I was not at liberty to
give his authority as freely as I may do
now. My dear friend died suddenly in
Baltimore last winter, and his son has,
I believe, succeeded to his post.

The magazine had a limited circula-
tion, but it reached Valerius Ebert,
whose voluminous letters were submitted
to Dr. Steiner, and returned, with anno-
tations. It also reached John Williams,
a soldier in Burnside's corps; and his
testimony is incorporated into the following sketch. It is valuable because
it shows the story of September 6th cur-
rent among the Rebels in Frederick a
few days after it occurred.

In 1887, Henry Nixtorf, a German
Unionist, — mentioned more than once in

my story, — published his " Recollections
of Barbara," through W. T. Delaplaine,
of Frederick. Although it contains some
interesting anecdotes, this volume adds
nothing to our positive knowledge, except the statement that the flag fluttered
from her " west window " as long as
Barbara lived.

There the matter seemed likely to rest,
until Mrs. Jackson published, last winter,
the Memoir of her husband, in which she
denies distinctly that there is *any founda-
tion* for the ballad. She asserts that she
makes this statement — and she does it
in evident good faith — after a thor-
ough inquiry in the city of Frederick.
Soon after this, Dr. Steiner passed away,
and I was at liberty to speak more
freely.

With the world in general, Mrs. Jackson's statement, mistakenly supposed to
refer to Barbara, will seem authorita-

tive; but Mrs. Jackson wished only to lift from her husband's brow the "blush of shame," with which the poet's imagination had remanded him to the "Legion of Honor."

In investigating the whole subject again, I have interviewed by letter or in person all those whom I originally consulted. Mrs. Handshew is still living, but too advanced in years to recall her story. I have got such information as I needed from the two brothers who originally told it, and at their suggestion I have had the local newspapers searched. During the Civil War there were two newspapers published in Frederick. An exhaustive examination of the columns of the Union paper has been made by Miss Diehl, of Frederick, extending over three years; but it has yielded only the account of Barbara's funeral, of which I copy here the conclusion : —

"Barbara removed to this city when a child. She remembered the signing of the Declaration of Independence, and the scenes of the Revolutionary War; she was familiar with the career of Washington, and shared the popular joy on the announcement of peace.

"In the quiet of domestic life she literally grew up with the nation's growth, and participated in its passing history; in middle age she witnessed the War of 1812; and when the sands of life ran low, she justly regarded the Rebellion, which now hangs like a cloud over the hopes of freemen, as the saddest experience of her protracted life.

"To one thus strangely identified with the origin and growth of the Republic, loyalty necessarily became a deep-seated sentiment; and when the Rebels were expelled from this city, on the memorable 12th of September, this venerable lady, as a last act of devotion, stood at her front door and waved the glorious star-spangled banner in token of welcome to our deliverers. On Sunday last her mortal remains were interred in the cemetery of the Evangelical Reformed Church, of which she was a consistent and exemplary member for more than forty years."[1]

I have corresponded with the present pastor of the church here alluded to, and it does not seem likely that any more detailed account of the events of September 6th will ever be accessible, unless, as has frequently happened in matters of greater moment, some dead soldier's diary should reveal it to posterity. Barbara Fritchie did not preserve the German spelling of her name, and I spell it here as it is spelled on her monument in the graveyard at Frederick.

CAROLINE HEALEY DALL.

1526 Eighteenth Street, N.W.,
WASHINGTON, D. C.

[1] From the "Weekly Examiner," Dec. 27, 1862.

BARBARA FRITCHIE.

PART I.

EVERYBODY in America knows the story of "The Man without a Country," and remembers how its author was beset with inquiries as to the real name and origin of the hero, Philip Nolan, who was born and lived in the imagination of Edward Everett Hale alone.

The experience is not peculiar. If in literature any author is so venturesome as to make use of a fact, its probability is at once questioned. If he give the rein to imagination, he is as speedily called upon for names and dates.

No one could help observing this in the Centennial year, for among the

many foreigners who visited Philadelphia, a large number travelled to Frederick to ascertain the whereabouts of
Barbara Fritchie; and during that summer the Northern papers teemed with
descriptions of the localities connected
with the purely ideal story of "Evangeline." Standing in the little cottage
attached to the Quaker almshouse in
Philadelphia, which was pulled down
that very summer, I saw a lady take
an old engraving from the shivering
wall and murmur, "I wish I knew
whether Evangeline ever saw this!"

The author of the ideal may well be
moved by any such tribute to his power;
but the man who idealizes the historic
must needs be vexed by the treatment
the world bestows upon his effort.

For myself, I offer no thanks to him
who attempts to turn William Tell into
a solar myth. He is mine, and I will

not give him up. So is the blind Homer of tradition, whether he were a poet in his own right, or merely a wandering harper who collected and chanted the epics of the past.

Moved by such feelings, in November, 1875, I published in the "New York Independent" a vindication of the truth of Whittier's story, drawn from antecedent probability, quoting in my own support a journal published by Dr. Lewis H. Steiner, of the Sanitary Commission, before the publication of Whittier's ballad. I had heard soldiers of both armies assert that they had seen old Barbara wave the flag; and as I did not know, at the time these assertions were made, that the story would ever be seriously questioned, as indeed I did not guess any question to be possible, it seemed best to restate the supposed facts in the lifetime of the author, and so challenge final confirmation or denial.

My article did very little good. In
the following May the Philadelphia
" Press " contained another on the opposite side. The point of this paper was
different from any I had attempted to
meet. The "Press" denied that a bullet
or volley of bullets cut away Barbara's
staff; and this is certainly true. But
does anybody care whether it did or
no? What I would assert is, that this
gray-haired woman, ninety-five years and
nine months old, stirred by the approach
of the Rebel army, mounted the short
stairway which led to her attic, and
waved her flag in the face of the advancing foe. It was the dim dawn of a September morning. No sympathetic Rebels
had crept out into the narrow street.
Only a few convalescents from the hospital watched the advance from the
bridge. The sight of Barbara raised the
coarse ire of some of the men, and their

lifted guns and uplifted voices were lowered at Stonewall Jackson's stern command.

Why is it that human hearts are so dead to the heroic? One would think that at the first glimpse of this noble story every eye would gleam, every bosom would throb with exulting sympathy! The ballad belongs to that class of poems which the world will never willingly let die. How does it happen, then, that so many persons are anxious to disprove, not merely the waving of the flag, but the very existence of Barbara Fritchie?

I will give a double answer to this question. I will tell the story as I understand it, as simply as if it had never been doubted; and then I will explain the state of things among her own relatives and townspeople, which made its denial possible in Frederick itself, —

Frederick, lifted into sudden illumination for Barbara's sake.

Many a time and oft had I desired to go to Frederick. Partly because it was a lovely little gem, set in a circle of historic hills, like Nazareth of old. Partly because Judge Taney was buried at the Jesuit Novitiate there, and I, a Protestant Abolitionist, had a tender feeling for this Catholic Southerner, now he was no longer able to fulminate unrighteous decisions, because he asked when dying to be laid next his mother Monica, whose body had been mouldering for more than fifty years in that cemetery. In Frederick also, under the shade of lovely cypresses, rested the body of Francis S. Key, author of the "Star-Spangled Banner;" and here also I meant to trace the fast-vanishing footsteps of Whittier's Barbara.

But when I was ordered into the

mountains of Maryland for my health, I forgot all these things. Ill of a low malarial fever, I went dreamily about the old town, gazing at the queer roofs where the shingles had a double lap which made them look like old Dutch tiles. Each shingle bound down not merely the one beneath it, but that on its own left; and the shadows ran up and down as well as across the roof. Dr. Steiner said that these shingles were of oak and hand-made, being thinned with a spoke-shave or a drawing knife towards both overlapping edges.

One day I was making a call in the friendly neighborhood, when I heard a bright young voice carolling to itself:

" Round about them orchards sweep,
Apple and peach tree, fruited deep."

" What ! " I exclaimed, " a saucy young rebel like you singing the story of Barbara Fritchie ? "

"There never was a Barbara," she pouted; "but the poet loved our Maryland!"

I went home and told this story. I was staying with dear friends, reputed Unionists. No one thought of blaming them because their sympathies were more than half with the land and people among whom they had been reared, rather than with the troops who had pillaged and oppressed them. I found that they too doubted the existence of Barbara, and then I spurred myself to inquire. It is pleasant to remember that one of the unbelieving ladies of the household went herself to Mrs. Handshew, and asked the questions which have made it possible to write this story.

I began to hear of relics, of the close-hidden flag, of oaken bits cut from the plank of the iron-wood stretcher over which Caspar Fritchie used to strain his skins. One night the delicate hand of a Southern lady sawed a bit of oak in two, and so divided for me her few inches of the door-sill over which Barbara's resolute foot had so often journeyed.

In the spring of 1876 there was living in Frederick a Mrs. Handshew, or more properly Handschuh. As far as I have been able to ascertain, Barbara had no blood-relatives living when she died; but Mrs. Handshew had been with her for some time, and nursed her in her last sickness. She was a niece of Barbara's husband, Caspar Fritchie.

Barbara left all her personal property to this woman, except her father's Bible; that she gave to a Mrs. Mergardt. This Bible is an ordinary quarto, very thick, and of a form familiar to most persons half a century ago. It is bound in calf; the sides are oak boards, and it was printed in German by Christoph Sauer, Germantown, Pa., in 1743. It is in good preservation, and the only writing in it is to be found on the inside of the front cover, where the following sentence is written in German : " This Bible belongs to Niclaus Hauer, born in Nassau-Saarbrucken, in Dillendorf, Aug. 6, 1733, who left Germany May 11, 1754, and arrived in Pennsylvania October 1, of the same year."

This inscription tells all that can now be known of the father of Barbara Fritchie. She never had a child, and no one of her husband's relatives knows her mother's name.

Barbara was born in Lancaster, Pa., where her father first settled, on the 3d of December, 1766, or one hundred and twenty-five years ago. He moved his family to Frederick much later. I could not ascertain the exact date, but from his connection with the Fritchies it seems certain that it was before the close of the Revolutionary War.

On the 6th of May, 1806, when she was nearly forty years of age, Barbara married John Caspar Fritchie, who was fourteen years younger than herself.

The service was performed in Frederick City by the Rev. Mr. Wagner, of the German Reformed Church. It would not have been at all singular if Barbara had never married; for although she was an active, capable woman, mistress of many generous enthusiasms, she had, as all confess, a sharp tongue. In his Report to the Sanitary Commission, printed in 1862, Dr. Steiner publishes a diary of the Rebel occupation of Frederick. Jackson's corps were recruiting, and under date of Tuesday, September 9th, he says, " A clergyman tells me that he saw an aged crone come out of her house, as certain

Rebels passed by, trailing the American flag in the dust. She shook her long, skinny hands at the traitors, and screamed, at the top of her voice, ' My curses be upon you and your officers for degrading your country's flag!' Expression and gesture were worthy of Meg Merrilies."

When Dr. Steiner sent me his report, he marked this passage, and told me privately that this was Barbara, three days after Jackson's men had fired on her flag. It is not likely that her spirit was less bold in her early youth, and I was a little curious to know why, if she married at that mature age, it must needs be a boy fourteen years younger than herself. I could learn only one central fact, — a fact honorable to Barbara and her family, and in keeping with what we know of her later life. The father of Caspar Fritchie had been a

Tory, sentenced by the laws of Maryland
to be " hung, drawn, and quartered, his
estates being confiscated."

The first part of this sentence was
executed. Owing to the intercession of
friends, probably of Niclaus Hauer himself, the confiscation was remitted, and
whatever property he had was given to
his widow to aid her in bringing up her
children. Caspar was born in 1780, and
it is likely that his mother died early,
for Barbara is said to have " brought up "
a brother and sister of her husband.

Caspar Fritchie became a somewhat
noted person in that locality. He was
a glove-maker ; and if Barbara did not
own the little cottage in which they
lived, he must have bought it and fitted
it up for his trade soon after his mar-
riage. It not only stood upon the very
edge of the creek which crosses the
principal street of the town and separates

tiny Frederick City from the Bentztown road, but the shop in which he worked overhung the creek, so that when he trimmed his skins, the clippings were swept through a trap into the creek itself. A sort of wooden balcony led back from the street across the end of the house to this shop, the balcony also projecting over the water. I am particular in describing this, because the fact that the house overhung the creek is the one circumstance which made her defiance of the Confederate army possible, even though that "army never passed through Frederick." Maryland, Kentucky, Pennsylvania, and Ohio all wanted the gloves which Caspar Fritchie made for riding, driving, and hunting. He was an excellent workman, and well known to his best customers, the gentry of the neighboring counties. He died in his seventieth year, Nov. 10th, 1849, thirteen

years before the wife who was so much
older than he that she might have been
his mother. His death left Barbara
very well off, but she did not change
her simple way of living.

Every afternoon she might be seen
sitting in the window of her little cottage, knitting-needles in hand. She
wore a black satin gown, with a clear-
starched muslin kerchief crossed over her
breast. She had a lady-like, quiet air.
Long before anybody had heard of a
photograph, Barbara Fritchie had her
daguerreotype taken. This picture
shows her between fifty and sixty years
of age, wearing a close cap and the
costume which I have described, and
which she never changed. She looks
very much like the traditional New
England grandmother, reared under the
shadows of the Puritan church; and the
first feeling that I had about the face,

was that it was very familiar, and not at all German.

Stern and somewhat cold she looked; but her eye was clear and true, and one saw in a moment how a little fun or a warm love might melt down the harsh lines.

She had living with her at this time and until her death, her niece, Harriet Yorner, more properly Jahner, born on the 4th of May, 1797. Barbara's first trouble after her husband's death grew out of her patriotic devotion to the Union.

Caspar Fritchie's will was drawn up by Dr. Albert Ritchie, of Frederick, who was also his executor. Barbara had only a life tenure in the estate, and after Dr. Ritchie's death in 1857, the laws of Maryland devolved the duties of administration upon his three nephews, the acting administrator being Valerius Ebert,

who turned out what Barbara called an
" arrant Rebel." Every time she received her dividends, they had some
sharp words. She had entered the last
decade of her century, and she wished to
live in peace ; so she went to one of the
oldest and most respected of the German
residents, the father of the late Dr.
Lewis H. Steiner, afterwards well known
in the Army of the Potomac as an active
inspector under the Sanitary Commission,
and at the last the highly prized librarian of the Enoch Pratt Library in Baltimore. The older Steiner was a shrewd
business man, and the " arrant Rebel "
asserts that Barbara had made savings
which she wished him to invest, "this being no part of the administrator's duty."

At all events, he was a conspicuous
member of Barbara's own church, — a
ruling elder. She begged him to take
her power of attorney and receive her

money.   Now, Frederick is a small city,
and even in 1876 it had many
cliques.   Its people are Northern as well
as Southern, German as well as English
born, Protestant as well as Catholic.
Mr. Steiner was very unwilling to inter-
fere, but he could not well refuse, so he
continued to transact Barbara's business
until his death.

Some time before the breaking out of
the war, he had a stroke of paralysis, from
which he entirely recovered.   Lewis, who
was either at college or the medical
school, and who had so far known very
little of his townspeople, was sent for to
attend him.   The first time Mr. Steiner
was able to walk out, he told Lewis that
he had some money that must be paid
to Frau Fritchie, and asked him to make
out a receipt for her to sign.

"Frau Fritchie" suggested to the
young student one of the old German

women whom he had often seen hoe-
ing in their gardens, and ignorant of
letters, so he not only made out the
receipt, but signed it in such a way as
to leave room for Barbara's "mark."

When his father ushered him into the
presence of the black satin gown and
starched neckerchief, he must have been
a little startled; but his heart did not
fail him. He courteously presented the
pen. Barbara took it, pushed back her
gold spectacles, and looked at the signature. "Bless you, honey," she exclaimed,
bending a humorous look on the young
fellow, "bless you! I wrote my name
as well as that long before you were
born!" and drawing her pen through
Lewis's signature, she wrote her name
firmly beneath.

I drew this story out of my friend
by asking whether he had not an auto-
graph of Barbara. "I have had a great

many," he said; "but I have kept only
this one, and nothing would induce me
to part with that;" and then he showed
me the receipt in question. I think it
was framed, and hanging on the wall
of his study.

In this way our Barbara lived, doing
her own work, with only Harriet Yorner
to help, until the war broke out, when
she must have been nearly ninety-five
years old. Then she found enough to
do in cheering and helping sick soldiers and despairing Unionists. She
went in and out of her own door many
times a day. If she found it difficult
to get up or down for the litter of idle
soldiers that cumbered the steps, she
was still strong enough to strike right
and left with her stout cane, shouting,
in Shakspearian fashion, "Off! off! you
lousy Rebels!"

In the winter of 1861 and 1862, when

things looked badly enough for the cause
of the Union, she went about helping
and cheering. Henry Nixtorf, a Lu-
theran, well known for sturdy piety and
patriotism, would tell with tears in his
eyes how, after every bit of bad news,
she would come into his shop, and strik-
ing the ground with her cane, cry out,
"Never mind, Harry, we *must conquer
sometime!*" This winter Barbara
bought a small silk flag, about eigh-
teen inches by twelve, not too heavy
for her aged arm to hold, while the
breeze that waved it, stirred also her
own memories of seventy-six. "It will
never happen," she was heard to say,
"that one short life like mine shall
see the beginning and the end of a
nation like this."

Harriet Yorner was sixty-five years
old when Barbara bought her flag, and
she was very timid, shrinking from the

sight of soldiers of either party. She
had reason enough to do so. The in-
habitants of cities like New York or
Boston have very little idea what the
residents of the little town of Frederick
were called upon to endure that winter.
Soldiers of both armies were constantly
in the way; a shot drew nobody to the
window, but drove timid people to their
hiding-places. Skirmishes and duels
were frequent in the narrow streets
which hands could almost stretch
across.

It was just before sunrise on Saturday, September 6th, 1862, that the
advance guard of Lee's army, under
Stonewall Jackson, came down the
Bentztown road. I do not mean that
the advance *entered* Frederick, — it certainly did not; but Stonewall Jackson
did. A little while before the troops
came within sight of Barbara's window,

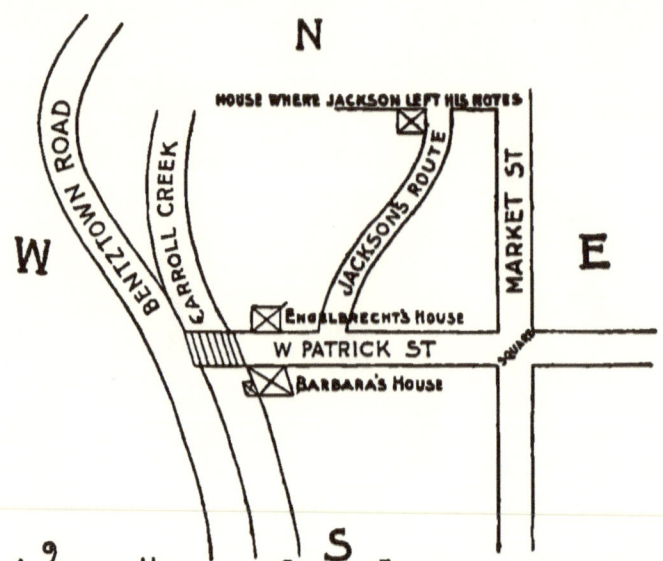

SKETCH OF HOUSE AND CITY OF FREDERICK FROM MEMORY.

the general dropped out of the line, and entering the town, thrust a little note under the door of a friend a few squares away. The note was simply to tell Dr. Ross, the Presbyterian minister, that he would meet him at church the next day. How he regained his position at the head of his command no one now living certainly knows, but it is not likely that he could penetrate the file crowding down the narrow road. Dr. Steiner asserted that he spurred his horse up a wide alley to Patrick Street, and that he was met by a townsman as he did so. Crossing the bridge built over the creek, he must have passed directly under Barbara's window. If the rudeness of his soldiers ever drew his attention, it was at this point, and here must his voice have rung out, " March on!" in the ears of his startled men. So much for the general's

part in the matter, by which I indicate the least he could have done.

How did it happen that the army did
not enter Frederick, if the general did ?
The question is easily answered. The
creek which ran by the end of Barbara's
house, and which in the olden time swept
away the trimmings of Caspar's skins,
forms the boundary between Frederick
City and Frederick County, of which
county that little town is only the
nucleus. Just across the creek is a
narrow lane called the "Benztown road,"
which makes an angle with the creek at
the bridge, and then sweeps along nearly
in a line with it.

For quite a distance before the army
reached the bridge, it must have been
visible from the attic window on the
west side of Barbara's house. It is not
likely that she had been asleep that
night. Everybody knew that the troops

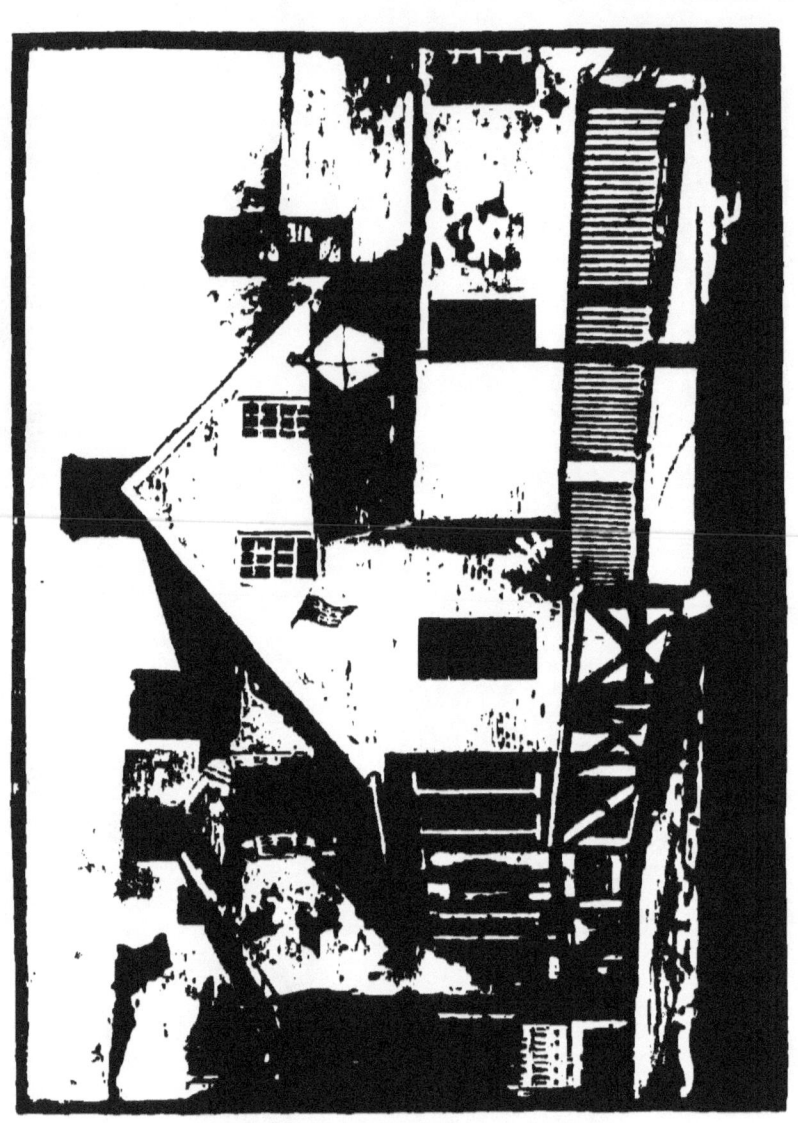

BARBARA FRITCHIE'S HOUSE.

From a Photograph taken by Byerly just before the house was taken down in 1868.

were on their way. She would be one
of the first to look out for Stonewall
Jackson. It has been said that she was
not able to leave her room at this time.
This was entirely untrue; but if it had
been otherwise, does not every woman
know what sort of strength it was that
would have carried her up that short
flight of stairs in the dim light of that
September morning, leaning on her well-
known staff?

The house consisted of a single storey,
with some attic chambers over it. Its
stairs were easy. The flag was already
in the window, as her friends assert, and
had been there ever since the previous
winter; and what happened while the
old woman stood beside it, soldiers on
both sides, men in the Confederate advance, and a few Union soldiers from
the hospital, have already told.

Harriet Yorner was saying her prayers

on the lower floor, with her face hidden behind Barbara's own bed, and got roundly scolded for her cowardice later, as she herself told Mrs. Handshew. Barbara was only doing as she had done ever since the war began. The Unionists of English descent were absolutely ignorant of and indifferent to the German population. It would be hard to tell what occasioned the bitter feeling which existed between the two races, if it were not for the fact that the Hessian mercenaries taken prisoner by our troops during the War of the Revolution were sent to Frederick. Some of them married there; and however their descendants may fare in the future, the Hessians were hated then, and the early German residents shared their fate. A few shots more or less made so little difference to Barbara that she was not likely to tell the story. In those exciting hours, one anxiety soon drove out another. That she stood by her flag, was insulted for doing it, as was certain to be the case in those days, and that the general himself came to the rescue, would seem sufficiently certain to whoever investigated the story on the spot, in the spring of 1876.

Who could have witnessed the scene besides the actors in it? Only the few convalescents from the hospital to whom I have alluded; for the houses of the citizens were not yet open, nor was Barbara visible to any one within the city limits. The story was told to Miss Dix in the hospital at Frederick, and on her return to Washington she confirmed it in a letter to Whittier.

Engelbrecht, the mayor of the little town at a later period, lived in a house on Patrick Street, directly opposite Barbara.

Prof. Samuel Tyler, the author of a Life of Chief Justice Taney, addressed some inquiries to the mayor as to the truth of this story.

In a letter dated June 30th, 1875, Engelbrecht replied in substance that he was at his own window when General Lee passed the front of Mrs. Fritchie's house, where his whole army halted while the advance under Jackson passed down the Bentztown road, and he saw neither Barbara nor her flag. Why should he? This was on Wednesday, September 10th, when the Confederates were leaving the town. Barbara confronted the advance on Saturday, September 6th, as it passed on to its encampment. Nor could Engelbrecht have seen her under any circumstances in his own house. The side window in the attic from which she waved her flag fronted the Bentztown road, and was invisible to any one at Engelbrecht's.

Professor Tyler, in communicating this to Miss Boyle, asserted that Stonewall Jackson did not pass Barbara's house, — and I willingly admit that he did not, on the 10th of September; but the professor then goes on to say that on that day he left the following note under the Rev. Mr. Ross's door on Second Street :

Regret not being permitted to see Dr. and Mrs. Ross, but could not expect to have that pleasure at so unseasonable an hour.

T. J. JACKSON.

Sept. 10, 1862, 5.15 A.M.

The note bore every sign of having been written in extreme haste. It was under this very door that General Jackson left another note on Saturday, September 6th, to say that he would be at church the following day; and this note Dr. Steiner saw an hour or two after it was written.

Now, Tyler's statement has nothing in

the world to do with our story. This
was Wednesday, and it was on Saturday
that the whole affair took place. Miss
Dix stated that Barbara's flag waved
from the attic window as long as the
Rebel army occupied Frederick. This
would not have been possible if it had
been the large flag, of which people
commonly think; but as the window did
not front the town, and the flag was so
small, it might easily have done so. Barbara had no reason to go to her front window on the day the army left. Her attic
commanded a complete view, not only of
the advance, but of the army that followed,— a privilege not shared, I believe,
by any other house within the town.

On Sunday, Sept. 7th, 1862, Stonewall
Jackson attended service at the Presbyterian church in Frederick, where Dr.
Steiner saw him; "and I am sure," added
the Doctor, in a letter to myself, " that he
worshipped with relish ! "

I saw every one in Frederick who
could be supposed to know anything of
the incident. Every one believed that
the flag had been fired upon, but it
is certain that no bullet struck the staff.
It is possible that one may have lodged
under the eaves; but although door-sill
and window-sill were cut into blocks
and treasured as relics, no one thought
of the bullet when the house was pulled
down. It is probable that Barbara's
story and Mrs. Quantrell's were con-
founded by rumor, for the staff of Mrs.
Quantrell's flag *was* cut away.

Two days after, Lee's army moved to
the west. On Friday, September 12th,
Burnside's army entered the very streets
of Frederick. The advance under Reno
crossed the bridge over the creek, entering between Barbara's house and one
opposite, where an old German clergyman, the Rev. Joseph Trapnell, himself

over ninety years of age, was waving his flag.

Barbara stood in the doorway of her house with Harriet Yorner and Mrs. Handshew. A younger member of the party, catching a glimpse of Mr. Trapnell, brought Barbara's flag from the house. Somewhat reluctantly, Barbara accepted and waved it. It was much more like her to shake her flag in the face of the advancing foe than to parade her good-will when a friendly army entered.

The groups in the two houses attracted the attention of General Reno. He saw at one glance the advanced age and the deep emotion of the two who held the flags. He halted between them. "Behold the spirit of seventy-six!" he cried out to his men; and they answered by a mighty shout, which echoed along the street.

This little incident, which has never been questioned in Frederick or out of it, spread the fame of the two old people throughout the town. It took place in full day, and was witnessed by both parties. The talk about it led the few persons who knew what had occurred on September 6th to speak of that also. The battle of "South Mountain" brought many wounded men into the hospital, and so the story slowly travelled. Whatever friends or relatives might know, they were little likely to boast of then, for outrage followed quick on loyalty. The close of September and the weeks that came after brought more than one event likely to shatter aged nerves. The 3d of December, which completed Barbara Fritchie's ninety-sixth year, found her in bed, which she had not quitted for a month, and where she was nursed by Mrs. Handshew and Harriet Yorner.

"Behold the spirit of seventy-six!" exclaimed General Reno; but he little knew how truly he spoke so far as regarded Barbara. When the Revolutionary War opened, she was old enough to enter into and understand it. When it ended, she was a woman grown. When Washington visited Frederick in 1791, Barbara sent some dainty teapot to be used in his behalf; and when the town of Frederick held funeral services in his honor, nearly ten years after, she was one of the pall-bearers, so early in her history had her steadfast patriotism become conspicuous.

All her life long she talked of the Boston tea-party and the success of the colonists, with loving pride, and the events of the Civil War kept the subject constantly in her mind. The glorious memory of what she had lived through stimulated her faith that the Union must survive. "We have seen darker times," she said frequently to Henry Nixtorf; and it is he who asserts that her flag floated from her west window until she died; nor does he believe that it was taken in between the 6th and the 10th of September. We have pretty conclusive evidence that it was still floating when, on the 13th of September, Mrs. Handshew went down into the flower-garden and left her to her encounter with the Union officer.

An account of this incident and of what occurred on the previous day, differing somewhat from that given to me by Mrs. Handshew fifteen years after, I will condense from a newspaper printed soon after the war closed.

"The troops were passing all day," Mrs. Handshew said. "I sent my daughter across the bridge to bring Aunt Barbara away; but she found her nodding and

laughing with the soldiers, and she
asked Julia to hand her a flag which lay
between the leaves of her Bible." It was
a little flag of twisted silk not two feet
long. *It had no staff*, — which may have
helped out the story of September 6th,
and Barbara waved it like a handkerchief.
" How old is grandmother?" said Reno;
and when some one answered ninety-six,
he reined in his horse, and three loud
cheers startled the air. He dismounted
and entered the house, and when he took
his seat, Barbara served him with wine
made by her own hands. The next day —
the very day on which Reno met his fate
at South Mountain — the Handshews,
who seemed to have lived just across the
bridge, spent the day with Barbara.
They went down into the garden to attend to some of her flowers, and when
she locked the door after them, they
charged her not to open it until they
returned.

" When we went back," said Mrs. Handshew, "she met us quivering with excite-
ment. 'I could n't help it, he would
have it!' she exclaimed. 'I did n't want
to give it, but he was a gentleman. He
had straps on his shoulders, and a gold
watch and chain.' At last she was per-
suaded to own that she had answered a
knock. Then an officer entered, and
pleaded so earnestly for a little cotton
flag that lay beside her that she could not
refuse it.

"' He would have it,' she kept repeat-
ing, 'but it was n't the one —'"

What did Barbara mean when she said
" that it was n't the one "? Probably
that the officer had asked for the flag
that she had waved on September 6th,
which was still fast in the west window
upstairs. This anecdote shows us that
Barbara had three flags, — one which told
the story of her loyalty to every man or

child that crossed the bridge, and which was finally bought by Valerius Ebert; one laid securely between the pages of her Bible, and held as sacred as the book itself; and a common cotton toy which was always in sight. It is probable that the officer was a convalescent at the hospital, about to rejoin his troops. If he be still living, these pages may fall into his hands. Is it too much to ask that he should speak?

Just opposite Barbara's house, and near the creek, a clear spring bubbled up; and as she went to and from Mrs. Handshew's, the soldiers crowded round her. If they were her " own men," her glasses and dippers were always ready; but if they were the " gray coats," her gold-headed cane stirred among them as if they had been dead leaves, and they scattered in all directions, driven by the curses that she did not spare.

On the 18th of December, 1862, three months and a half after her trembling hand had shut the attic window down upon her little flag, she peacefully breathed her last. In the graveyard of the Evangelical Reformed Church the curious traveller will find two marble headstones, surrounded by a wall of evergreens, bearing the inscriptions : —

JOHN C. FRITCHIE,
Died Nov. 10, 1849, aged 69 years.

BARBARA FRITCHIE,
Died Dec. 18, 1862, aged 96 years.

When the funeral was over, and the Rebels were rid of "Brave Barbara," the "mayor and corporation" had a double reason for trying to get possession of the little house in which she had lived. In the first place, and in spite of what has been said to the contrary, so many inquiries had already been made concerning Barbara that they were glad to cut them short by saying, with apparent truth, " There is not a house in town which ever belonged to any such person."

On the other hand, the little creek was a dangerous foe to the town, and had more than once swamped the cellars and lower storeys of the houses in its neighborhood in a way that not only threatened disease and death, but that induced worthy citizens to consider their taxes and the amount to be paid yearly to retrieve personal losses. So the corporation bought Barbara's house, and pulled it down.

Fortunately for us, Barbara had one relative who was not ashamed of her, and who knew very well that her little flag had been waved in the sight of the whole world, although she might not have suspected it.

This was a certain John D. Byerly, photographer, who called his workshop at 29 North Market Street, Frederick, a studio, and refused to send anything out of it that did not please him. If nobody knew anything of Miss Dix's story at the time of Barbara's death, how did it happen that this man made haste to copy the old daguerreotype?

I have said that Barbara left all her personal property to Mrs. Handshew. If she gave her the flag with all the rest, there was one man in town shrewd enough to offer its price.

Mr. Byerly knew where to find it, and in spite of the Southern sympathies of its owner, he borrowed it, set it in the west window where it had waved from the time that Barbara bought it until shortly before her death, and photographed the little house before the corporation pulled it down.

When it was levelled, about two thirds of the lot was dug away, so that the wicked creek might find room enough for its sudden vagaries; and on the remaining third a small tinshop was erected, which was still standing in 1878. Harriet Yorner survived her old friend. She died at the age of seventy-seven, on the 1st of May, 1874. Her story, as connected with that of Barbara, rests on the word of Mrs. Handshew, who was living when I went to Frederick. Harriet was buried in the quiet yard at Frederick, where her body was laid beside those of Barbara and Caspar.

If my story be true, what were the motives to the various contradictions and denials connected with it?

How peremptory these were, the following anecdote will show : —

In the month of May, 1876, I went into a druggist's shop in Frederick to get a little quinine. It was Sunday morning, and while I waited, a stranger sauntered in, wearing the gray morning coat of the conventional Englishman.

" Will you tell me, sir," he asked of the druggist, " whether a woman named Barbara Fritchie ever lived in this town ? "

" Certainly," was the answer.

" Ah ! " responded the Englishman, stroking his whiskers with an air of relief, " there is evidently a mystery. I asked at the hotel : they said there was no such person here. I replied that she might be ·dead, but there must be a grave, relatives, or at least the house in which she had lived ; but the landlord angrily denied that there was any such thing. I determined not to leave town without inquiring on the street, and as it is Sunday and the shops are shut, I must trouble you." The druggist explained. The traveller could not wait for Dr. Steiner, who had not risen, and it ended in my leading him to the bridge and into the solemn shadow of the evergreens at the cemetery while the druggist put up my powders.

The owner of the hotel turned out upon inquiry to have been a personal enemy of Barbara. I think it is not difficult for the reader to see how little likely Barbara was to boast of her defiance to her friends, or tell of it in any way to her husband's nephews. As far as she was concerned, she contented herself, according to Mrs. Handshew, by scolding Harriet Yorner for her cowardice. The denial was given partly in ignorance, and partly in unsympathizing disgust, while the Anti-Union feeling was still strong. Once given, it must be adhered to.

If it be asked why the leading Unionists of the town said nothing about it,

I would reply that the incident occurred at a time and place when no one
but Jackson and his men could be expected to know of it. To Jackson it was
but one of a hundred similar incidents
and small disturbances connected with his
march, the only peculiarity being the extreme age of the woman. Six days after
Barbara's achievement, the wife of one
of the prominent Union men in Frederick
unfurled her national flag — a much
bigger one than Barbara's — just as
Stewart's men dashed by her house.

"It was pleasant and fitting," Dr.
Steiner says in his diary, "that a member
of the Washington family should so have
welcomed the incoming Union troops."

But there was a still stronger reason.
When I asked the niece of Admiral
Goldsborough, who divided her oaken
relic with me, why she, a Union woman,
had never heard this story, she answered

at once, "Because we never had anything
to do with the Hessians." The prejudice
which separated the old Union residents
from the Germans seemed to have been
stronger than that which divided them
from their Rebel neighbors.

I once heard a Union officer assert in
a railway car that he had seen a shot
fired at Barbara's flag. It was in November, 1868, between Baltimore and Washington; and I was on my way to the
colored schools at Beaufort. His statement was not made in controversy. It
was perfectly simple. He described the
position of the house accurately, railing
somewhat profanely because the corporation had so unnecessarily destroyed the
house, instead of widening the creek on
the side of the Bentztown road. I listened
intently and looked at him with great
interest, but did not ask his name, because at that time I did not know that

it was possible to doubt the story. Both Harriet Yorner and Barbara died before it was questioned.

Who are the persons who have denied this story over their own name?

1. Mayor Engelbrecht, an honest man and a Unionist, but one who made a mistake in the time alluded to. It was on Wednesday, September 10th, not Saturday, the 6th, that he stood all day at his upper window watching the main body of Lee's army as it passed. But if it had been on the 6th, he could not have seen Barbara, for her own house would have been interposed between herself and him.

2. A certain Samuel Tyler, lawyer, and author of the Life of Judge Taney, who died in 1878. He relied first upon the mayor's statement, and next upon the fact that Jackson's forces "did not enter Frederick." He started with the

mistaken idea that Barbara was said to wave her flag from the front window, and so had no motive for telling us how close the Bentztown road came to Barbara's side window, or for recalling the fact that Stonewall Jackson attended church in the town the next day.

3. A Bangor paper, dated, I think, Jan. 26, 1876, denies the story on the authority of " one of the family." Upon inquiry this turned out to be the "arrant Rebel " with whom Barbara would have nothing to do.

4. A more elaborate denial was made by a writer calling himself " Karl Edmund," in the Philadelphia " Press " on the 18th of May, 1876.

As his letter was written after a visit to the spot, it is as well to advert to his objection that Dr. Steiner did not publicly stand by the story. That a German Unionist living in Frederick City should feel it unnecessary to take sides on this matter in the midst of far more important duties, will surprise no one who has been there long enough to recognize the vestiges of the old feud, or to sympathize with the social predicament in which the close of the war found some of its best citizens.

The story was certainly told while Barbara lived. It was openly gossiped over in the hospitals as soon as death released her from annoyance. It became public in the following year.

Karl Edmund suggests that a Mrs. Quantrell, " now in Washington," might have been the true heroine. Such a person may have waved a flag on the 10th of September, when Lee went out of town, or when Burnside entered; but no house in Frederick but Barbara Fritchie's had a window that confronted Jackson's advance on the 6th.

5. The most important denial is one said to have been given recently by a member of Jackson's staff residing at Hagerstown. If the reader will turn to the account of Jackson's absence of a few moments only from the head of the advance, he will see that it need not have been observed by any of his staff.

The officer is of course correct when he denies that Jackson gave the order to "Fire!" As no one now knows at what part of the column the disturbance occurred, it may easily have escaped the notice of any one man.

The whole story turns on local peculiarities that have been wholly ignored in the telling.

No one asks how it was that a story to which there were so few witnesses became instantly linked to Barbara's name. Jackson's men remained in the neighborhood four days. The few sol-

diers or hospital patients who witnessed
the scene had many opportunities to ask
who lived in the little house overhang-
ing the creek. Everybody could tell,
and the story was never doubted till it
became hopelessly entangled in double
dates and mixed motives.

The poem is historically true to the
spirit of the loyal woman who gave
it being. In several minor respects it
errs, for the history of the 6th of
September had not then been written.

" All that day through *Frederick street*
sounded " *no* " tread of marching feet,"
and the marching in the *county* ceased
at an early hour. It was not noon,
but daybreak, when Barbara mounted
to her attic. Stonewall Jackson *never*
ordered his men to fire on the flag
held in an aged woman's hand. He
was not at the " head" of his advancing column. The moment he reached

it, he did indeed give the order to
" March on ! "

So far I had told the story in my
article of April, 1878. When I wrote
to Whittier, asking for a copy of Miss
Dix's letter, he was not able to find
it ; and although Mrs. Southworth's
seems to have been printed soon after
the ballad was written, I have seen only
that portion of it which is quoted by
Karl Edmund in May, 1876.

It was Mrs. Southworth who first told
the story to Whittier, and *she* did not
attribute to Stonewall Jackson the orders
to " halt and fire " which make part of
Whittier's poem. If she thought, not
living in Frederick, that such an order
had been given, it was natural that she
should have supposed a " volley " followed, and that Jackson gave the order ;
although we have every reason to sup-

pose that only one or two irregular shots were fired. Miss Dix's whole soul exulted in the story, for she was quite capable herself of the action it recorded, and was glad to confirm it. Whittier, knowing nothing of the details, told the story in his most heroic mood ; and the song will live longer than the facts.

Up to the time that I published the result of my investigations, Valerius Ebert, who was that nephew of Caspar Fritchie from whom Barbara refused to receive her dividends, had made no public statement concerning Barbara. In April and May, 1878, I received several letters from this nephew, chiefly filled with slanderous charges against Dr. Steiner. When I humorously reported these to the Doctor, he replied, after characterizing the man somewhat broadly, as follows :

"Once, during the occupancy of our place by some United States cavalry under General Stahel, at the request of his distressed wife I rescued Ebert from the rough hands of some of the troops. Of course he is grateful! I am sorry he has a poor opinion of me!"

Some time after, a copy of " The Journal," a Sunday newspaper printed at Evansville, Ind., on April 14th, 1878, was sent me. In this, a letter from Valerius Ebert asserts that at the time Lee's advance entered Frederick, Barbara was lying in her bed, a helpless invalid within a few weeks of her death.

Now, we know this is not true, for six days after the advance, Reno's men cheered her upon her front porch, where she again waved a flag, and " was seen of many."

His next assertion is that Ebert never had a sharp word with his aunt; and against that we must set the statement of Dr. Lewis H. Steiner and his father, to whom Barbara went for relief, — well-known persons both of them. Then comes the amazing assertion that, as a politician, Aunt Barbara "was never demonstrative." Every German resident in Frederick knew better than that. Nothing would be gained by copying Ebert's letters to me, and I pass on to one of greater interest.

The April number of "Sunday Afternoon," in which I published my first account of Barbara Fritchie, was issued about the 10th of March, 1878, according to the very reprehensible modern practice of anticipating the proper date, — a practice which will make newspapers and magazines historically worthless to the succeeding generations. Soon after that date, I received the following letter from one of Burnside's men. It answers very fully the statement that the main fact of Barbara's story was never heard of in Frederick during her life : —

No. 712 Rhode Island Avenue,
Washington, D. C., March 16, 1878.

Madam, — I have read this day with great
interest your *capital* article in the April
number of the " Sunday Afternoon," entitled
" The Truth about Barbara Fritchie." I
also remember reading your article on the
same subject published in the " Independent "
sometime in 1875. And now, let me tell
you what *I* know about this famous act of
" Dame Barbara's : " —

On the 18th of September, 1862, the day
after the battle of Antietam (and twelve
days after Barbara is said to have confronted
the advance), I happened to be in Frederick
City with several of my comrades belonging
to Burnside's Ninth Army Corps. We were
in search of a glass of beer, and were shown
a little house where it was said that we
could procure it. We entered, and found a
very pretty Irish girl in charge; and after
some " persuasive logic " she introduced us
to a barrel of lager, and we had a good time.
I remember very well her telling me the
story about Barbara Fritchie and the flag.

We were very much interested, and under the inspiring influences of the moment, the writer paid his compliments to the great "Stonewall," after which the pretty maiden shouted, "Bully for Jackson!" I at once retorted, "If you say that again, I'll kiss you!" But I did n't, for she hastily withdrew, leaving "the boys" in command.

On our way to the front we called to see, and did see, Barbara Fritchie's house; and I am willing to make affidavit to the same. But you have told "the truth, the whole truth, and nothing but the truth."

Very respectfully,

JOHN WILLIAMS.

CAROLINE H. DALL, care of "Sunday Afternoon," Springfield, Mass.

Now, it is obvious that the value of a letter like the above depends upon the character of the man who wrote it. At the time I received it, I had no thought of publishing it. Since the issue of the "Life of Stonewall Jackson," I have seen the necessity of reasserting all that part of the story that relates to Barbara's heroism, of explaining how the poet, naturally ignorant of the history of the day and the character of Stonewall Jackson, most innocently attributed to him an order, which, under no circumstances, could he have been induced to give.

I think it probable that, however well the story was known, Jackson was never credited with the order to " Fire ! " until after the ballad was published, in October, 1863. I therefore determined to find John Williams, who had heard the story twelve days after the incident occurred, and ascertain exactly what was said about the general when the little Irish girl told the story. But, alas ! I found only his grave.

The War Department could not help me, because I could not properly define his position. It then occurred to me that fourteen years was not a very long time, and that I might trace him from the house where he had lived in 1878. His family were remembered, and it was easy for me to find his widow, who has recently married a second time. The little sketch of his life which follows, I took down from her lips and from papers in her possession : —

John Williams was born in Cornwall, at St. Just, a parish in the western part of Penzance. He reached this country in time to receive a certificate of citizenship in Jackson, Michigan, in 1860, and on the breaking out of the war, enlisted in the Eighth Michigan Infantry and served as quartermaster. In 1865, after the war ended, he seems to have entered the service of the Freedman's Bureau. He went to the Carolinas, and finally to Jackson, Miss., carrying teachers to the colored schools.

He finally settled in Mississippi, and became "reader and librarian" to the Mississippi Senate, — a title which his widow
insisted upon, although it sounded oddly
to my New England ears. The office
corresponds to our "clerk of the senate." He came to Washington in 1877,
and obtained a clerkship in the Treas-
ury, where he remained until his death
in 1886, at the early age of fifty-seven.

Some resolutions, passed by his com-
panions in the Sixth Auditor's Office,
were framed and hanging on the wall.
They spoke of his careful and accurate
habits. His death was instantaneous.
He fell as he left his room in the morning; and the resolutions stated that
no unfinished work was left on his desk
the night before, and that his papers
were as carefully filed as if he had
known what was to happen. They
spoke also of his generous heart, his

genial smile and ready wit. I found his wife very proud of his college education, his wide reading, and personal refinement. The Senate of Mississippi passed resolutions at the time of his death, which were sent to his brother, a prosperous citizen of Penzance. I have thought it worth while to recapitulate his story, because it gives the impression of a man who could be trusted.

If I could find the Union officer who said he saw the shot fired at the flag, I think the evidence of Barbara's heroism would now satisfy a court of justice.

CAROLINE HEALEY DALL.

1526 Eighteenth Street, N. W.,
    WASHINGTON, March, 1892.

PART II.

BARBARA'S HOME AND ITS NEIGHBORHOOD IN 1876.

I HAVE said that it was the niece of Admiral Goldsborough who divided for me the bit of oak that had been cut for her from Barbara Fritchie's threshold; and when I name her, many a United States soldier will rouse himself to read, and many a Northern mother of dead sons will breathe a blessing choked by sobs. It was she who talked to me of Frederick. Quaint, indeed, I found the old town. It really seemed to consist of but two streets hardly a mile long, crossing each other at right angles, and so making a market square in the centre, and intersected in odd ways by narrow lanes, through one of which Stonewall Jackson was seen to spur his horse on the morning of Sept. 6th, 1862.

A few miles away flows the Potomac, hidden by a low mountain wall between which and the town were the broad pastures and orchards "fruited deep." Fair, indeed, it was "as a garden of the Lord." The conical summit of the "Sugar Loaf" cuts the clear blue sky, and showed no remnant of the Stars and Stripes that once floated aloft. The Presbyterians still called their congregation together by a sharp-voiced *triangle*, and every quarter of an hour the old town clock rang out the time, telling by repeated strokes how many quarters had glided away.

On the outskirts you can still trace the barracks built for Braddock's men, and used as a prison during the Revolutionary War. As I dwelt on these things, Miss Goldsborough said, —

"But you ought to go to the Novitiate. Father McElroy is the oldest Jesuit in the world."

So it happened that the next day I went over to the Novitiate. When I was shown into the dusky ante-chamber to await the coming of the priest, I was stirred to the very depths; for out of its dim shadows I seemed to see approaching the form of a long lost friend. I lost him out of the dancing-school and the old dining-room in Bowdoin Square, where we had studied our Greek verbs together.

Joseph Coolidge Shaw went to Europe from Harvard College. When he became a Jesuit priest at Rome, he sent home a portrait of himself in a priest's robes, and after his death his family sent it to the institution which had

sheltered his last hours. His life had
been one of fearless truth, mingled with
the sweetest devotion and self-denial.
If I had ever known that he died here,
I had lost sight of the fact. The
darkness of the alcove in which the picture hung, hid the frame and the back-
ground. I seemed, as I entered, to
encounter the living form that I had
loved.

Father McElroy had long been blind;
but even to his consciousness my per-
turbed feeling was soon revealed. He
asked for an explanation, and when I
gave it, sent for the nurse who had
tended my friend in his last illness,
who went with me to the grave which
I had never expected to see, and told
me many a lovely anecdote of the steps
which led to it. Father McElroy could
not talk long enough of one who had
been a favorite pupil, and while we
pondered, the hours sped.

The old Father had been born in 1781.
He had just celebrated his ninety-fifth
birthday. For three years he had been
totally blind ; but with what a cheerful
voice he answered my inquiries ! " ' The
Lord gave, and the Lord hath taken
away.' So much may I say with holy
Job !" and then he went on to tell
me of the beautiful October days which
he had seen in Frederick, with gay sun-
shine glinting through the bright-col-
ored leaves.

He had been a dear friend of Cheve-
rus, and sat at his side at that historic Boston dinner when the bishop,
finding himself opposite to William El-
lery Channing, bowed to him and said :

" You see, they have set orthodox and
heterodox over against each other !"

Father McElroy gave Father Byrne
a key that he might take me into the
church opposite the Novitiate. " When

I came here in 1803," he went on to say, " we had but one bishop in the United States. This church, which I built, was only the second in the country, and for a long time the handsomest. In 1823 all the bishops came to consecrate it. There were only eight. Now we have more than sixty, and the Catholics constitute one seventh of the population of the United States. *Then* there were three millions of people in the country; *now* there are forty. Never in the world has the Church seen such an increase as this! "

The church which Father McElroy built is indeed a fine one. It was he who secured its precious pictures. The altar is of white marble, and a magnificent painting of the Crucifixion hangs above it.

Father McElroy was three years a chaplain in the Mexican War, attached to Taylor's command. At its close he was sent to Boston, where he built the Jesuit College and the Church of the Immaculate Conception. It was not till he was nearly blind that he was allowed to come back to the city of his love. He died in the summer of 1877, at the age of ninety-seven.

It was a sunny Sabbath afternoon when — a few days later — I drove out over South Mountain. Braddock's road crossed mine almost at a right angle. A spring is still shown where his men stopped to drink. The hillsides are covered with chestnuts hung with vines. From the latter the Germans make a very fair claret. From the cemetery where Francis Key's body was laid, one may look far down the road which leads to Washington. It is a broad highway, traversing the distance with a mighty sweep. As I looked, I felt as if the poet's dry bones must have put on their flesh when the Rebel army marched into Frederick!

Old De Vol, who had charge of the cemetery, had been on the spot all through the war. He saw Burnside enter, — the sun gleaming on his bayonets, cavalry skirmishing along the road, and the artillery throwing shells from the rear over both armies. I could see it all as I listened and looked down the turnpike, threading the beautiful hills on the way to Georgetown! When you are on the spot, Harper's Ferry also seems to be only a suburb of Frederick. Certainly, John Brown and dear old Barbara have long since shaken hands!

Mᴀʀᴄʜ 14, 1892.

PART III.

THE BALLAD.

(The words in italics are intended to indicate assertions
that are mistaken.)

Up from the meadows rich with corn,
Clear in the cool September morn,

The clustered spires of Frederick stand
Green-walled by the hills of Maryland.

Round about them orchards sweep,
Apple and peach tree fruited deep,

Fair as a garden of the Lord
To the eyes of the famished rebel horde;

On that pleasant morn of the early fall
When Lee marched over the mountain wall, —

Over the mountains, winding down,
Horse and foot into Frederick town.

Forty flags with their silver stars,
Forty flags with their crimson bars,

*Flapped in the morning wind; the sun
Of noon looked down and saw not one.*

Up rose old Barbara Frietchie *then,*
Bowed with her fourscore years and ten;

Bravest of all in Frederick town,
She took up the flag the men hauled down;

In her attic-window the staff she set,
To show that one heart was loyal yet.

Up the *street* came the rebel tread,
Stonewall Jackson riding ahead.

Under his slouched hat left and right
He glanced; the old flag met his sight.

*" Halt ! " — the dust-brown ranks stood fast ;
" Fire ! " — out blazed the rifle blast.*

*It shivered the window pane and sash ;
It rent the banner with seam and gash.*

*Quick as it fell from the broken staff,
Dame Barbara snatched the silken scarf ;*

She leaned far out on the window-sill,
And shook it forth with a royal will.

" Shoot, if you must, this old gray head,
But spare your country's flag," she said.

A shade of sadness, a blush of shame,
Over the face of the leader came ;

The nobler nature within him stirred
To life at that woman's deed and word.

"Who touches a hair of yon gray head
Dies like a dog !   March on!" he said.

All day long through *Frederick street*
Sounded the tread of marching feet;

All day long that free flag tost
Over the heads of the rebel host.

Ever its *torn* folds rose and fell
On the loyal winds that loved it well;

And through the hill gaps sunset light
Shone over it with a warm good-night.

Barbara Frietchie's work is o'er,
And the rebel rides on his raids no more.

Honor to her! and let a tear
Fall for her sake on Stonewall's bier.

Over Barbara Frietchie's grave,
Flag of freedom and union wave !

Peace and order and beauty draw
Round thy symbol of light and law;

And ever the stars above look down
On thy stars below in Frederick town.

JOHN GREENLEAF WHITTIER.

COMMENT ON THE ITALICS.

WHETHER forty flags flapped in the morning air was of little importance; the point to be made is that Barbara did not raise her flag at *noon*. She went up to the window, where it had fluttered for months, because that was the only window that commanded the advance, and it was at five o'clock in the morning.

The troops came, not *up the street*, but along the Bentztown road; and as I say elsewhere, Stonewall Jackson was *not at their head*. Trusting to the quiet of the town, he had left them, to do an errand of his own.

The irregular firing set up by the angry soldiers did not *shiver* either *pane* or *sash* or *staff;* it simply dislodged the staff, when Barbara seized it and waved it, with the noble words the poet quotes.

All that follows, until we come to Jackson's order, " March on ! " is of course unhistoric, and later the flag must not be described as *torn.*

When I first got to the bottom of the facts, I thought the poet might conform to history by altering a few lines of the ballad. But I soon saw that this could not be done.

We must leave the ballad as it is. Stonewall Jackson will not suffer, and Barbara would have confronted him and a " volley " from his troops with the immortal courage Whittier describes.

C. H. D.

NOTE. — Mrs. Jackson's denial will be found in the " Life and Letters of Gen. T. J. Jackson," issued by her through the Harpers, in New York, 1891.

L'ENVOI.

WHEN I corrected the first proof of this little volume, I hoped to carry it happily to Whittier, in the beautiful home at Hampton Falls, where he has passed, as he lately said, "the happiest summer of his life." With that home my childish steps had been familiar. In its old garden, made sacred now by his vanishing presence, I had found, long years ago, the reddest currants, and picked the ripest plums.

Alas! I have brought, not my completed work, — but let me drop one leaf into this open grave: I cannot drop a flower. Why have we gathered in this old orchard with our hearts aflame? Why have gentle and simple crowded the Amesbury streets and looked

searchingly into the faces of the incoming crowd, to see if we are worthy of
the noble company we have kept?

The heart of New England has been
moved as never before.

During the last ten years this generation has parted with almost all those
who made our common life beautiful
and dear.

Statesmen, soldiers, orators, poets, and
lovers of mankind, precious to the common heart, have passed behind the veil.
Our tears are even now falling for one
whom Whittier loved, — Curtis, the
gracious, the serene, the all-helpful, who
never touched his pen save to move a
human soul or right a public wrong.
So bitterly and so often have we sor-
rowed that we have grown callous to
our pain.

Why, then, does this last parting touch
us to the quick?

It was the glorious function of Whittier to lift us nearer to the Infinite Spirit, to keep us intent upon our immortal destiny, and to fill us with that love of Beauty which is the love of God. Every line of his is instinct with spiritual life; and it is so of no set purpose, only because it was not in him to withhold himself.

"He has entered into eternal life." Did some one whisper that? Nay, he was born into that life! Its "clouds of glory" encompassed his first conscious being; he knew from the beginning his infinite inheritance, — "Because I live, ye shall live also." We feel this in his verse and in his life. It is an open lesson. What has been deepest in ourselves has responded to his inspired touch. We loved him because he glorified life, exalted duty, and brought us face to face with God. This is the inevitable function of any artist, be he poet or painter, who is to leave an immortal memory. Vice, crime, and the loathsome slime of distorted lives are transient. He who lives to depict these, whether with pen or brush or chisel, shall pass from human consciousness as they pass.

The Immortal is the uplifting, the All-Holy alone. We are told that we have had honest politicians, honest lawyers, honest merchants, honest preachers; but in Whittier we had that "noblest work of God," — *an honest man.* His integrity was vital. It did not appertain to any function, to any casual occupation or utterance. It was the man himself, and met in its entirety every emergency of our national or individual life. He thought exactly and promptly; as he thought he spoke; as he spoke he lived; and for his thought he could

7

easily have died, had God asked him to do so.

This is my leaf. Let it fall, not only into this open grave, but, folded in my words may it not also fall into some young, warm, human hearts, — hearts that are not yet old enough to miss those who have been the glory of our generation, but which the future may kindle into a divine emulation ?

"Here let me pause, my quest forego:
Enough for me to feel and know
That He in whom the cause and end,
The past and future, meet and blend,
Guards not archangel feet alone,
But deigns to guide and keep my own."

What of our friend ? What cheer hath he ?
"Where lingers he this weary while ?
Over what pleasant fields of heaven
Dawns the sweet sunrise of his smile ?

"Still, on the lips of all we question,
The finger of God's silence lies:
Will the lost hands in ours be folded,
Will the shut eyelids ever rise ?

"O friend! no proof beyond this yearning,
This outreach of our hearts we need;
God will not mock the hope He giveth,
No love He prompts shall vainly plead!"

AMESBURY, MASS., Sept. 10, 1892.

www.ingramcontent.com/pod-product-compliance
Lightning Source LLC
Chambersburg PA
CBHW032201010726
47493CB00008BA/2776